Shirley Barber's

The
TOOTH FAIRY

The Five Mile Press

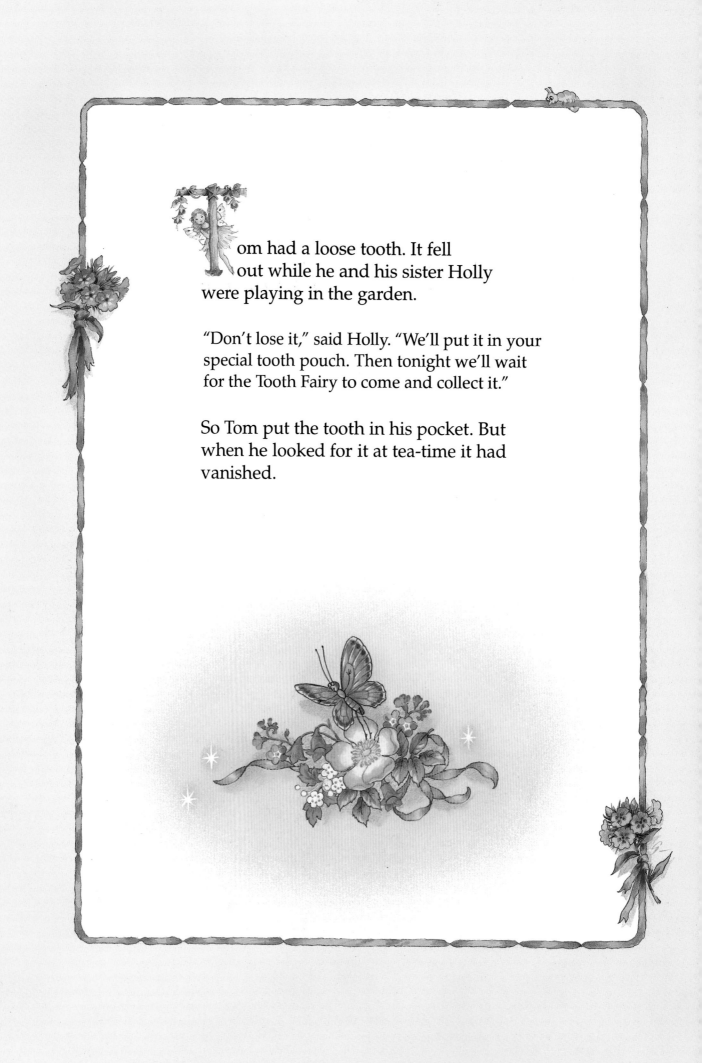

Tom had a loose tooth. It fell out while he and his sister Holly were playing in the garden.

"Don't lose it," said Holly. "We'll put it in your special tooth pouch. Then tonight we'll wait for the Tooth Fairy to come and collect it."

So Tom put the tooth in his pocket. But when he looked for it at tea-time it had vanished.

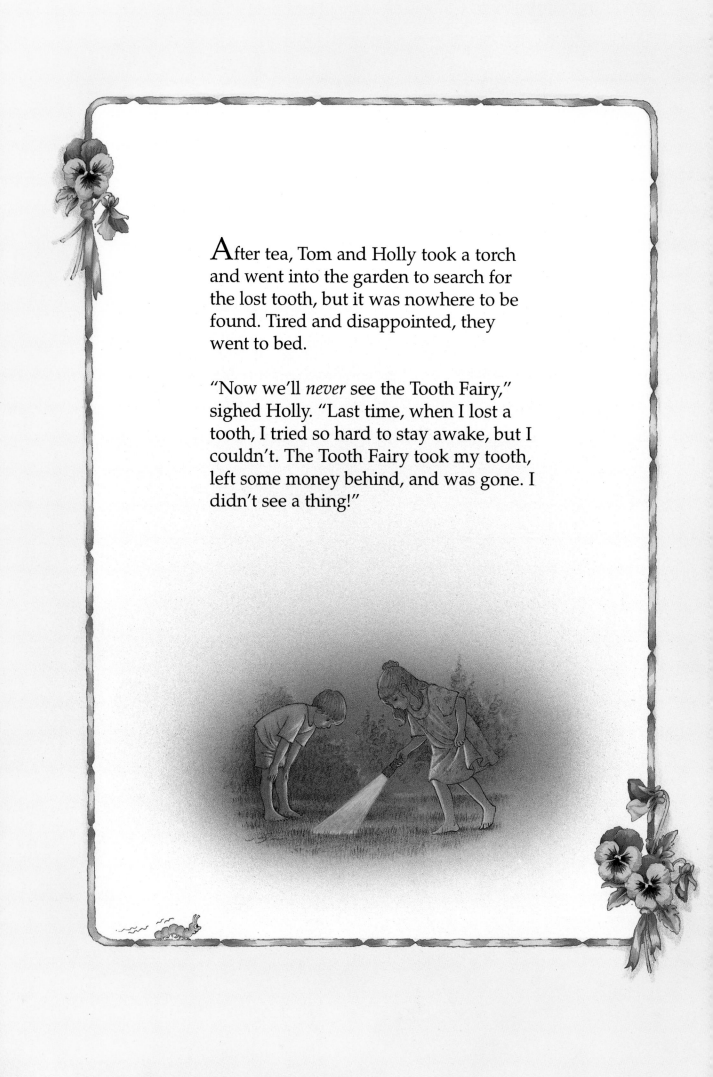

After tea, Tom and Holly took a torch and went into the garden to search for the lost tooth, but it was nowhere to be found. Tired and disappointed, they went to bed.

"Now we'll *never* see the Tooth Fairy," sighed Holly. "Last time, when I lost a tooth, I tried so hard to stay awake, but I couldn't. The Tooth Fairy took my tooth, left some money behind, and was gone. I didn't see a thing!"

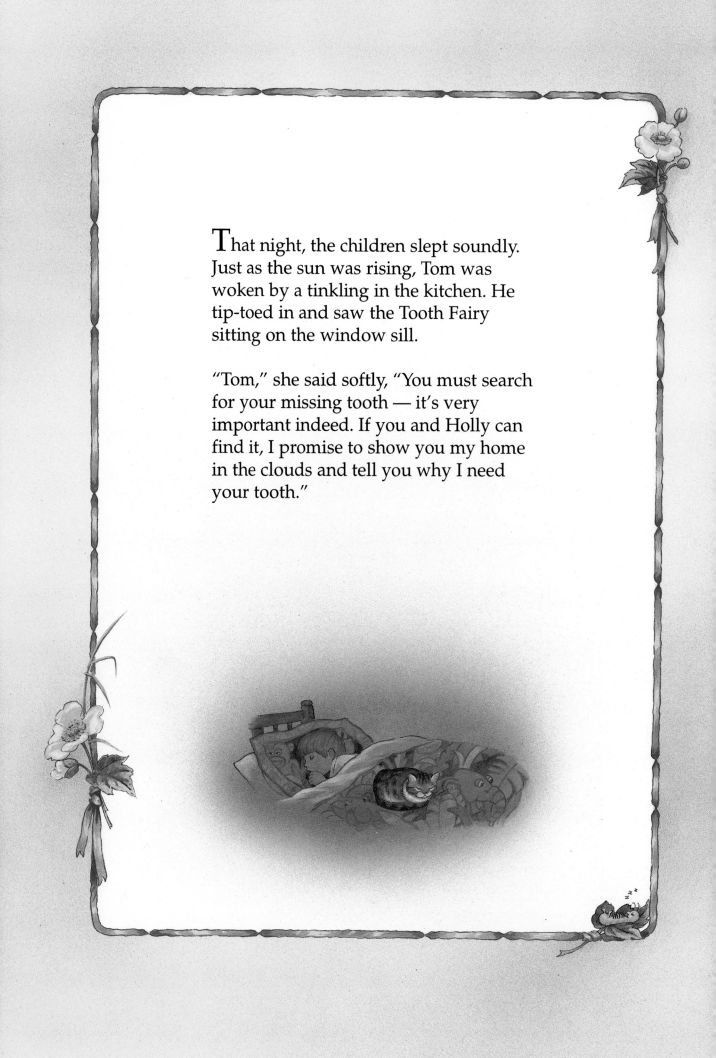

That night, the children slept soundly. Just as the sun was rising, Tom was woken by a tinkling in the kitchen. He tip-toed in and saw the Tooth Fairy sitting on the window sill.

"Tom," she said softly, "You must search for your missing tooth — it's very important indeed. If you and Holly can find it, I promise to show you my home in the clouds and tell you why I need your tooth."

So Tom woke up Holly, and together
they ran out into the garden. Frantically,
they searched for the missing tooth.

At last, they found it, shining white
amongst the daisies.

"Hooray!" laughed the Tooth Fairy.
"Now I'll take you to Cloudland, just
as I promised."

She waved her magic wand, and suddenly
Holly and Tom were as small as the Tooth Fairy.

But before they had time to be surprised, she
waved her wand again and white doves began
to swoop down from the trees. They had golden
bridles and red velvet saddles.

"Jump on, Holly!" cried Tom. "We're going for a
ride — up into the sky!"

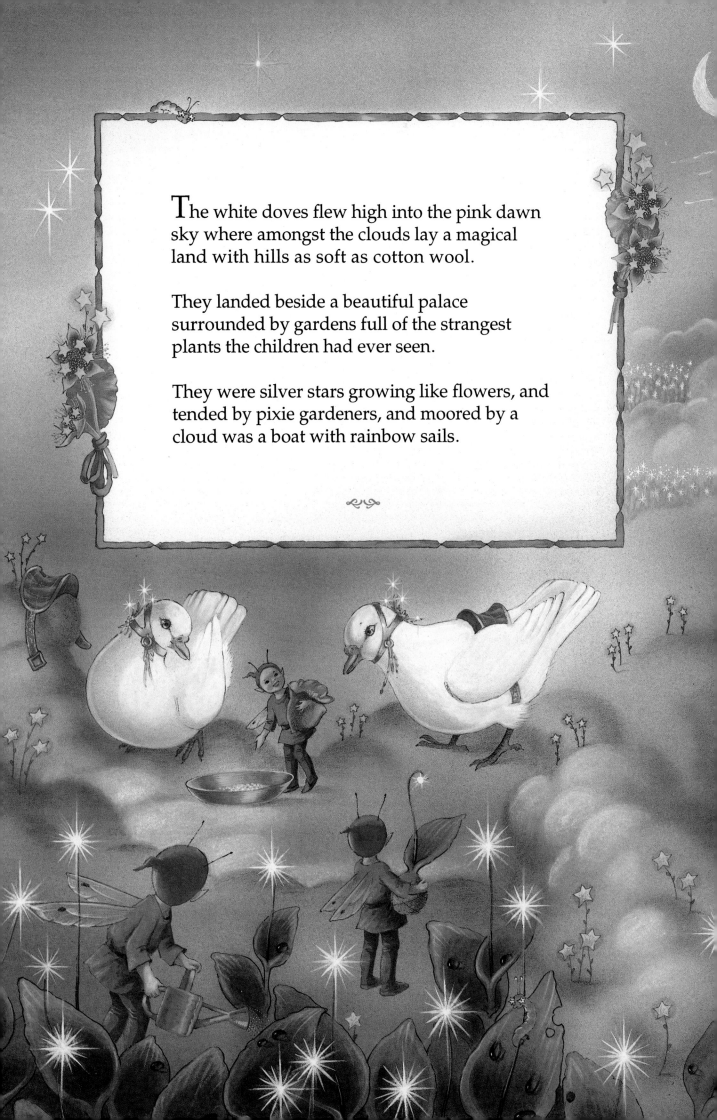

The white doves flew high into the pink dawn sky where amongst the clouds lay a magical land with hills as soft as cotton wool.

They landed beside a beautiful palace surrounded by gardens full of the strangest plants the children had ever seen.

They were silver stars growing like flowers, and tended by pixie gardeners, and moored by a cloud was a boat with rainbow sails.

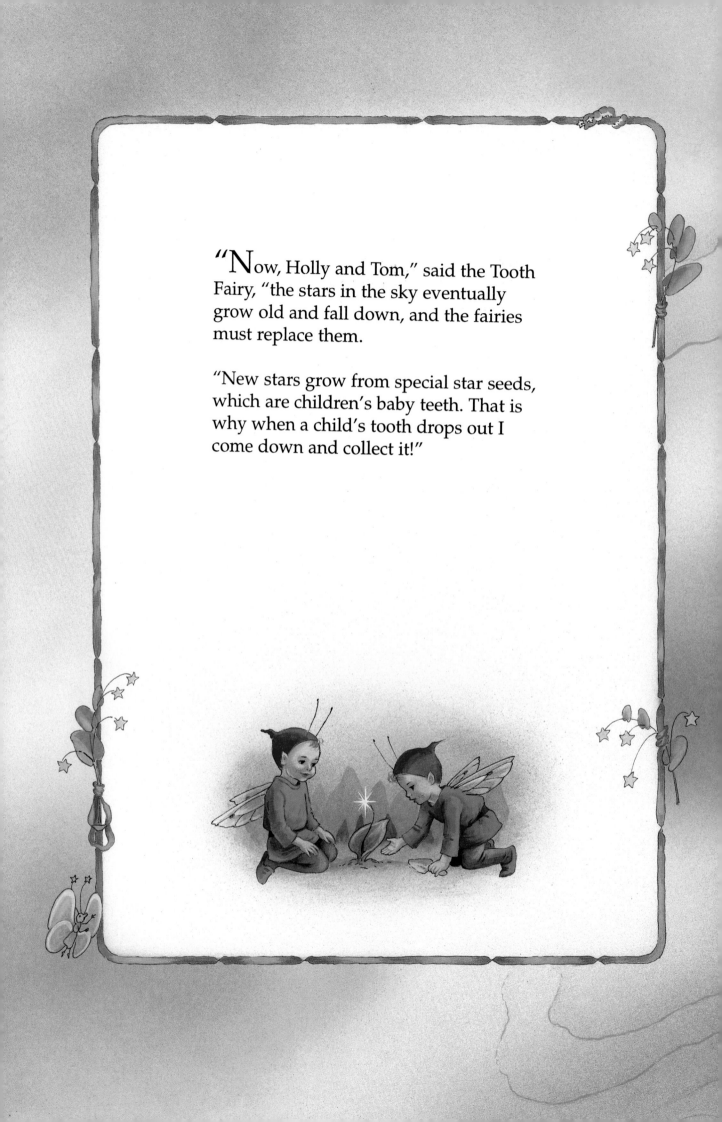

"Now, Holly and Tom," said the Tooth Fairy, "the stars in the sky eventually grow old and fall down, and the fairies must replace them.

"New stars grow from special star seeds, which are children's baby teeth. That is why when a child's tooth drops out I come down and collect it!"

"But why is my tooth so important?" asked Tom.

"Well," said the Tooth Fairy, "most stars in the sky are silver, but here and there you can see gold ones.

"Now, *your* teeth are very special, Tom, because they will grow into golden stars. And we know an old golden star will fall very soon, and will need to be replaced."

"Look!" cried Holly. "A golden star is falling now!"

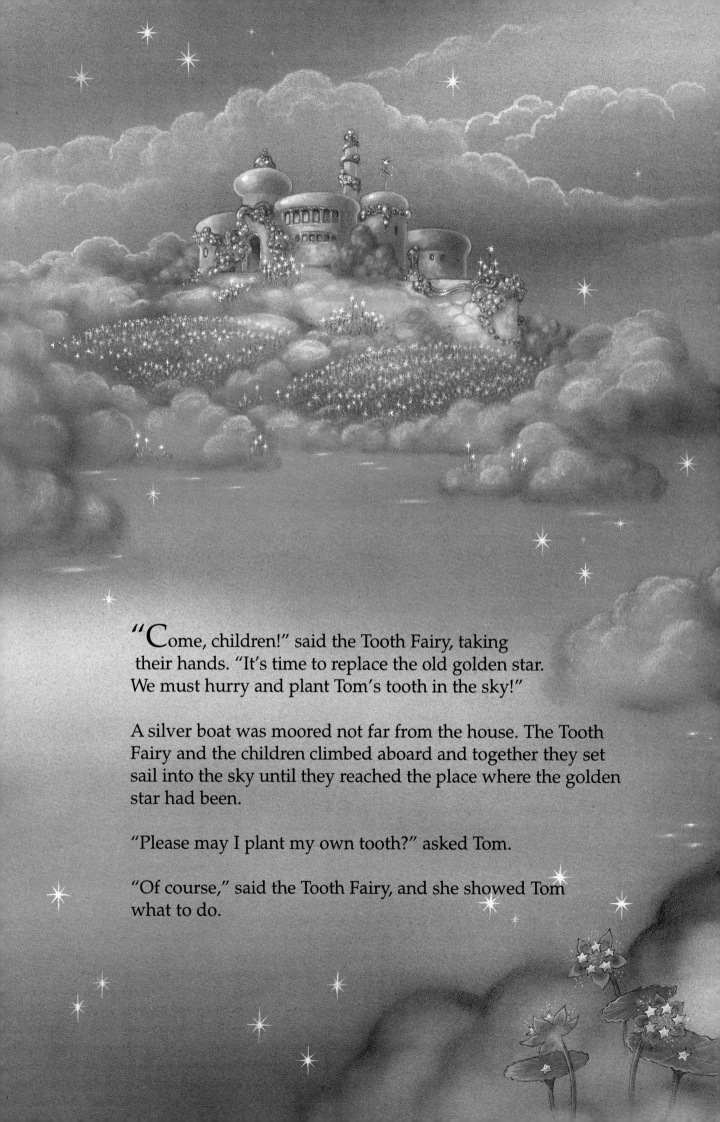

"Come, children!" said the Tooth Fairy, taking
their hands. "It's time to replace the old golden star.
We must hurry and plant Tom's tooth in the sky!"

A silver boat was moored not far from the house. The Tooth
Fairy and the children climbed aboard and together they set
sail into the sky until they reached the place where the golden
star had been.

"Please may I plant my own tooth?" asked Tom.

"Of course," said the Tooth Fairy, and she showed Tom
what to do.

The silver boat sailed back to
Cloudland, and the Tooth Fairy and the
children jumped out onto the clouds.

"Soon you must go home," said the
Tooth Fairy, "but first come into my
house and have some breakfast."

A bell tinkled and all the pixie gardeners
came scampering inside to join them.
They all had breakfast together. Then
the Tooth Fairy waved her magic
wand and...

Tom found he was back in his
own bed!

Holly came running into his room.

"Tom!" she said excitedly. "Did we really
see the Tooth Fairy last night? Or was it
a dream?"

"It's true!" laughed Tom. "The Tooth
Fairy took us with her to Cloudland!"

That night, Tom and Holly searched the
sky for a glittering new golden star.

"Look!" cried Tom, at last. "There it is!
That's the one I planted! My very own
golden star!"

The Five Mile Press

The Five Mile Press Pty Ltd
950 Stud Road, Rowville
Victoria 3178 Australia
Phone: +61 3 8756 5500
Fax: +61 3 8756 5588
Email: publishing@fivemile.com.au
Cover design by Sonia Dixon

First Published 1995
Reprinted 1997, 1998, 1999 (three times), 2001 (twice), 2003

Copyright © Marbit Pty Ltd
Illustrations and text by Shirley Barber
All rights reserved

Printed in China

National Library of Australia
Cataloguing-in-Publication data
Barber, Shirley
The Tooth Fairy

ISBN 0 86788 866 0
ISBN 0 86788 867 9 (pbk.)

I. Title
A823.3